MCR
16.00

MCR

JAN 1 0 2007

EVANSTON PUBLIC LIBRARY

P9-CRO-502

9 1532

Yolen, Jane.
Baby Bear's books /

DATE DUE	
APR 1 5 2007	OCT 1 1 2007
APR 2 6 2007	
JUN 0 5 2007	JAN 0 4 2008
JUL 0 2 2007	JAN 2 5 2008
	MAR 2 0 2008
JUL 1 0 2007	APR 2 3 2008
	MAY 1 1 2008
JUL 2 1 2007	
AUG 1 5 2007	
SEP 0 5 2007	

DEMCO, INC. 38-2931

JAN 1 0 2007

BABY BEAR'S BOOKS

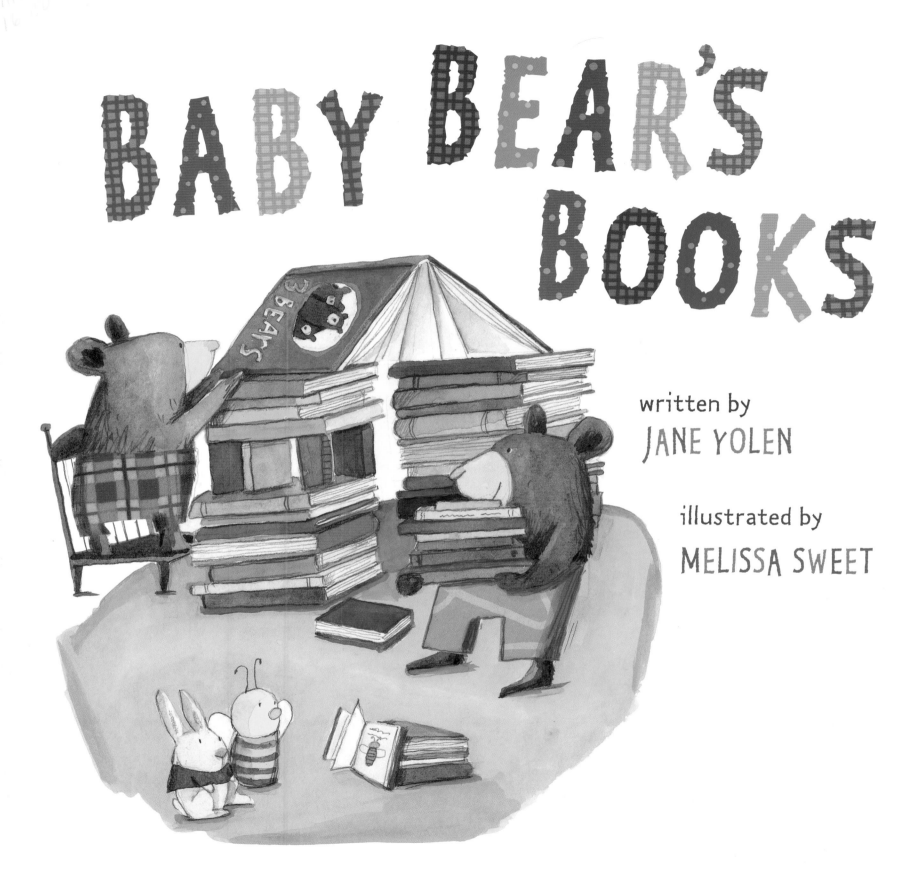

written by
JANE YOLEN

illustrated by
MELISSA SWEET

HARCOURT, INC.

Orlando   Austin   New York   San Diego   Toronto   London

EVANSTON PUBLIC LIBRARY
CHILDREN'S DEPARTMENT
1703 ORRINGTON AVENUE
EVANSTON, ILLINOIS 60201

Text copyright © 2006 by Jane Yolen
Illustrations copyright © 2006 by Melissa Sweet

All rights reserved. No part of this publication may be reproduced or transmitted
in any form or by any means, electronic or mechanical, including photocopy, recording,
or any information storage and retrieval system, without permission in writing
from the publisher.

Requests for permission to make copies of any part of the work should be mailed
to the following address: Permissions Department, Harcourt, Inc.,
6277 Sea Harbor Drive, Orlando, Florida 32887-6777.

www.HarcourtBooks.com

Library of Congress Cataloging-in-Publication Data
Yolen, Jane.
Baby Bear's books/written by Jane Yolen; illustrated by Melissa Sweet.
p. cm.
Summary: Throughout the day, Baby Bear finds a book to fit every special moment.
[1. Books and reading—Fiction. 2. Day—Fiction. 3. Bears—Fiction.
4. Stories in rhyme.] I. Sweet, Melissa, ill. II. Title.
PZ8.3.Y76Baar 2006
[E]—dc22   2005019203
ISBN-13: 978-0-15-205290-4   ISBN-10: 0-15-205290-9

H G F E D C B

Printed in Singapore

The illustrations in this book were done in mixed media
and collage on watercolor paper.
The display and text type were set in Kosmic.
Color separations by Colourscan Co. Pte. Ltd., Singapore
Printed and bound by Tien Wah Press, Singapore
This book was printed on totally chlorine-free Stora Enso Matte paper.
Production supervision by Ginger Boyer.
Designed by Scott Piehl

To wee David, who loves books—J. Y.
To Kirsten, who loves books—M. S.

When I wake up
and before I am fed,
please, will you read
while I sit on the bed?

The first book's a wild book.
My day has begun
with bears bouncing madly
and having much fun.

I know all the words,
so I'll say them right out.
I'll whisper and growl them,
I'll giggle and shout.

So, read to me stories
of happy and after,
big books that all end with
a lot of bear laughter.

Now it is snack time,
some honeycomb, please.
Will you read something
here under the trees?

Snack time's the right time
for hearing a tale.
A story, like honey,
can never get stale.

Maybe a tale
of a bear in a den,
with houses of candy
and gingerbread men.

Or read something gentle
and happy and sweet.
We'll snuggle real close
on the old garden seat.

I'll sit and I'll read—
only pictures, not words.

I'll read to big brother,
my bee...and the birds.

Nap time's all dozy,
a soft, cozy time.
So, onto your lap
I will carefully climb.

And there you can read me
a wave-rocking tale,
as off into faraway
dreamland I sail.

So, read me a book
about bears in cold streams,
as over the wavelets
I go in my dreams.

One book, then two
till I'm deep in my nap,
cuddled and cradled
in Mama's warm lap.

Now it is dinnertime.
As Mama cooks
I want to hear more
about bears in my books.

Read to me books
about big bears who eat,
and drop all their food
on the floor at their feet.

Read to me books
where the bear is a king
yet Mama Bear makes him eat
every last thing.

Read to me books
where Papa Bear bakes,
and dinners all end
with some huge honey cakes.

Now after my bath,
when I'm ready for bed,
here's the best time
for a book to be read.

I'm into my jammies.
I've turned on the light.
I'm snuggling down,
and I'm ready for night.

My eyes start to close,
but my ears open wide.
So, come and sit down
with a book by my side.

Then read to me spaceships
and bear trips and then,
when you are finished...

Oh, read them again....